# I'm Adopted!

by Shelley Rotner and Sheila M. Kelly

photographs by Shelley Rotner

Holiday House / New York

Special thanks to Marla Allisan, JD, LICSW,
and Full Circle Adoptions, and to Angela Baptista
for the photograph on page 23 (left).

Text copyright © 2011 by Shelley Rotner and Sheila M. Kelly
Photographs copyright © 2011 by Shelley Rotner
All Rights Reserved
HOLIDAY HOUSE is registered in the U.S. Patent and Trademark Office.
Printed and bound in April 2011 at Kwong Fat Offset Printing Co., Ltd.,
Dongguan City, China.
The text typeface is Breughel.
www.holidayhouse.com
First Edition
1   3   5   7   9   10   8   6   4   2

Library of Congress Cataloging-in-Publication Data
Rotner, Shelley.
I'm adopted! / by Shelley Rotner and Sheila M. Kelly ; photographs by Shelley Rotner. — 1st ed.
p. cm.
ISBN 978-0-8234-2294-4 (hbk.)
1.  Adoption—Juvenile literature.
2. Adopted children—Juvenile literature.
I. Kelly, Sheila M. II. Title.
HV875.R655 2011
362.734—dc22
2010029561

To the parents and children who made this book possible
by sharing their stories and agreeing
to be photographed, thank you.

S. R. & S. M. K.

Children can bring joy to a family.

When people are
unable to make a baby,
or choose not to,
they can adopt one.

Lots of children
are adopted.

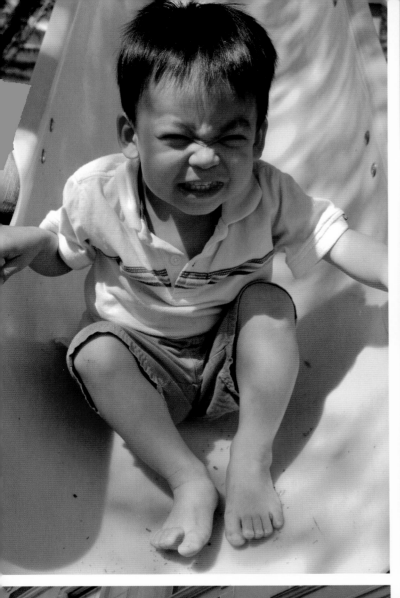

Parents who want to adopt get help to find just the right child . . .

to care for and to love.

When adoption day arrives, everyone celebrates . . .

parents, grandparents, brothers, sisters, and friends.

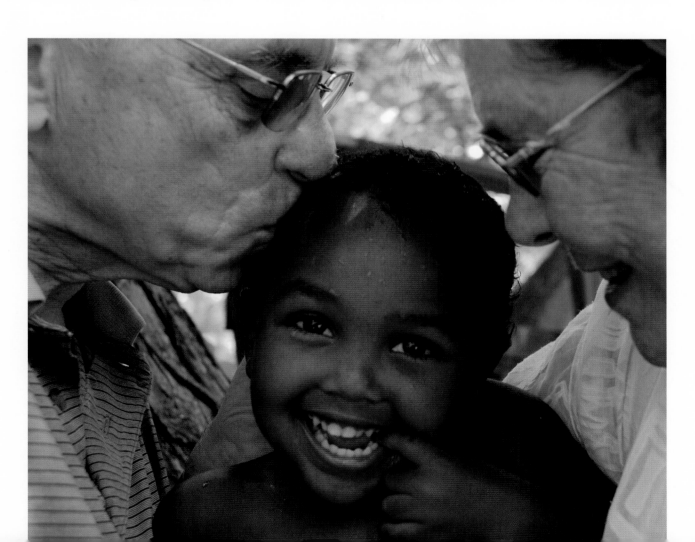

Mothers love their babies, but sometimes
a mother is unable to care for her child.
It may make her sad to have her child adopted.

Usually, adopted children want to know
why their birth mothers could not keep them.

There are many reasons.

It may have been because she was too young and had no one to help her

or was too poor to buy food, medicine, and clothing for her child.

It may have been because the father or mother became sick,

or their country was made dangerous by a war.

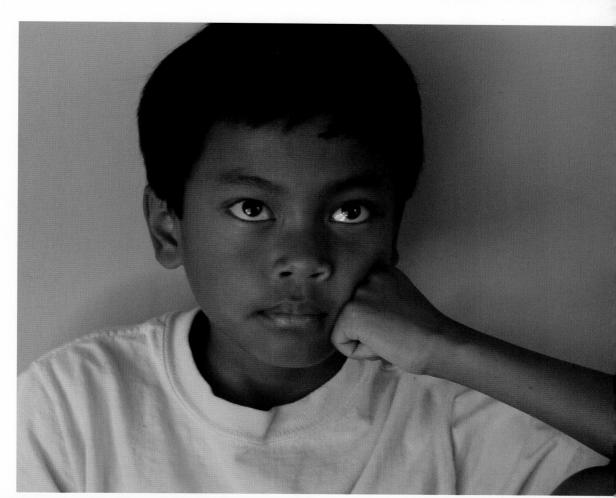

Some adopted children come from this country.

"I was born here.
My parents went to
the hospital to get me."

Others come from far away.

"I came here on an airplane."

"We did too."

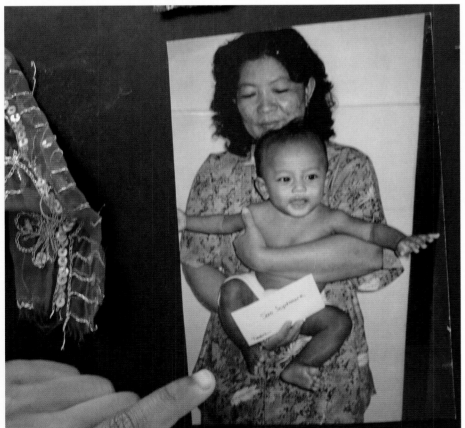

Adopted children often want to know about the country where they were born.

"We have pictures."

"Where I was born, people speak a different language and look different from most people here."

Families often visit the place where their adopted child was born.

Sometimes adopted children look different from the other members of their families.

"I don't look like my sister, but
we like to do the same things."

"I'm not the same
shade as my mother."

Children are happy in their families,
no matter where they were born . . .

when they know they are cared for and loved.

Most children want to hear the story of how they came to their families.

"Tell me
about the day
I came home."

They want
to hear it again . . .

and again.

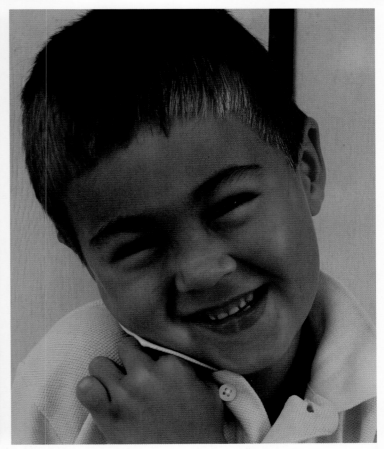

The authors acknowledge that every adoption is unique,
and there are adoption arrangements not described in this book.

There are, for example, "open" adoptions in which plans are made
to keep the birth parent or parents in contact with the child.
There are also occasions when both birth parents make the decision
to have their baby adopted. There are cases, too, when children are
adopted during adolescence.

We have chosen to depict the most typical adoption stories in this book.

S. R. & S. M. K.